From the Movie

Disney

FROZEN
MAGIC OF THE NORTHERN LIGHTS

LET IT GLOW

Written by Suzanne Francis

Illustrated by the Disney Storybook Art Team

PaRRagon

Bath • New York • Cologne • Melbourne • Delhi
Hong Kong • Shenzhen • Singapore

Autumn was nearly over, and Little Rock and his friends were on a journey to the trolls' crystal ceremony. Each year the leader of the trolls, Grand Pabbie, honours all of the young trolls.

Little Rock couldn't wait to get there! But to be part of the ceremony, Little Rock had to prove himself by finding Grand Pabbie and earning his tracking crystal. Elsa, Anna, Kristoff and Olaf had promised to help their little friend find his leader.

"I bet there is a great clue just around the bend," said Kristoff.

Little Rock smiled. "Let's get tracking!"

Little Rock hunted for clues as the group headed up the mountain. Suddenly, he noticed a funny-looking bump under the snow.

He quickly dug down deep.

"Look!" he said, popping up with an axe and a rope.

"So that's where they were," Kristoff said. He had lost his axe and rope last spring!

"I tracked some important stuff," said Little Rock.

"You *found* some important stuff," said Kristoff, placing the items into Sven's saddlebag. "That's not tracking. Remember?"

Little Rock nodded. He had made the same mistake before. Tracking was a difficult skill but Little Rock needed to work it out. Otherwise, his tracking crystal would never glow.

"But you did show inventive thinking," said Anna. "And that's one of the rules of tracking, right?"

"Yes!" Little Rock answered. "Along with fearlessness and observation."

Kristoff smiled. "Would you like to hear a story about how I was inventive, back when I was young?"

Little Rock nodded again. So, as they began hiking, Kristoff started his story.

"When I was a child, Sven and I were out harvesting ice one night. The Northern Lights were very bright and they were reflecting on the surface of the frozen lake. Sven was going crazy trying to catch the reflections.

"He carried on chasing them for a while until he finally caught one ..."
Kristoff paused before adding, "with his tongue!"

Sven groaned in embarrassment while everyone else giggled at the story.

"He was completely stuck.

"So I tried pulling him ...

... and pushing him,
but nothing worked.

His tongue just stretched and stretched.
I reached for my ice pick, but he didn't like that idea!

"I'm just not very good at tracking." Little Rock held up the dull
crystal and sighed. Then he explained that he would never have found
Grand Pabbie without his friends. "If anyone here has earned a tracking
crystal, it's all of you. Not me. I needed you, my friends, to get here."

Suddenly, Little Rock's tracking crystal started to glow!

"Look!" said Anna, pointing at the shimmering crystal.

"But I didn't earn it," said Little Rock.

Grand Pabbie nodded. "Actually, you did. You worked out what it takes to be a good tracker." For Little Rock, that meant understanding that he needed help from his friends. And that realization made the crystal glow!

Just then the other young trolls came out of hiding, cheering,
"Hooray for Little Rock!"

Grand Pabbie and the trolls had been waiting for Little Rock to
find them and earn his final crystal. Now it was time for the crystal
ceremony to begin.

As Grand Pabbie called for all the young trolls to gather around him, Little Rock looked shyly at his friends. "Oh, I need my other crystals now," he said.

Little Rock's friends had been keeping his other crystals safe – just in case he lost them on the journey. Kristoff gave back the water crystal. Then Anna, Elsa and Olaf handed over the crystals Little Rock had earned for learning how to be fearless and observant.

With the glowing stones in his hands, Little Rock joined the other young trolls around Grand Pabbie.

As Grand Pabbie lifted his arms into the air, all the trolls raised their crystals. The Northern Lights reflected the colours of the crystals, and the lights bounced back into the sky slightly brighter. But not as bright as Grand Pabbie had hoped.

"Mind if I try something?" Elsa asked.

Elsa waved her arms and her magic curled into the sky, creating a giant snowflake. It sparkled as it turned, reflecting the Northern Lights back into the sky and all around them!

Olaf hopped with excitement. "It's a rainbow!" he gasped.

Elsa and Anna's dresses shimmered, too.

"Well, now," said Grand Pabbie. "That is so much better!"

Far away, in Troll Valley, the grown-up trolls looked up at the amazing colours in the sky. Thanks to the young trolls, the Northern Lights were shining strongly again. And everyone knew what the bright lights meant: Little Rock had succeeded in his quest!